100 PEOPLE

MASAYUKI SEBE

Here are

It's time to start

100 people.

playing hide-and-seek!

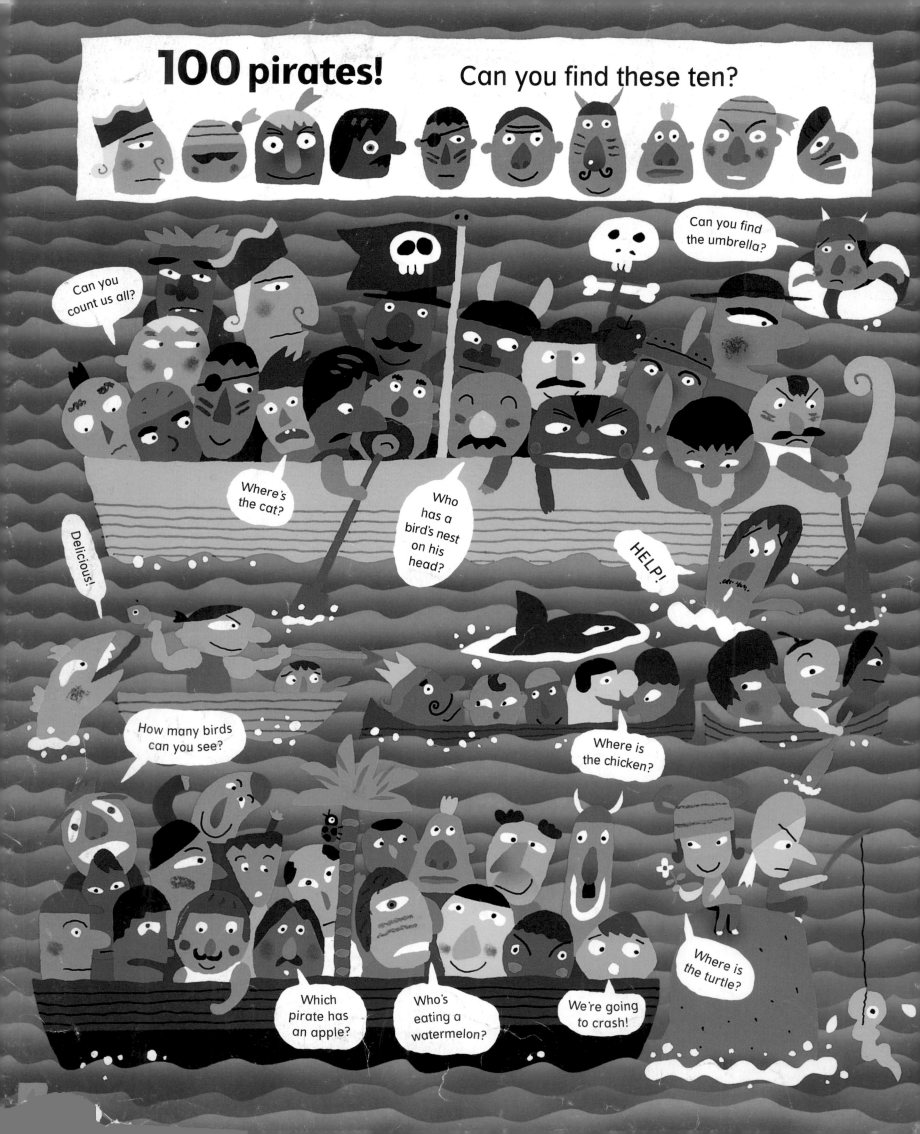

100 faces!

Can you find these ten?

Has anyone seen my banana?

Who's doing a handstand?

How many chicks can you see?

6

7

100 kings!

Can you find these ten?

Where's the fox?

Wow! I can see an emperor with no clothes.

Can you see the dog?

Look at all our golden crowns!

Which king has an apple?

100 kings! Can you count us?

HELP!

11

100 lookalikes!

Can you find these ten?

100 Father Christmases! Can you find these ten?

100 runners!

Can you find these ten?

100 diners!

Can you find these ten?

20

100 children!

Can you find these ten?

23

Can you find these ones too?

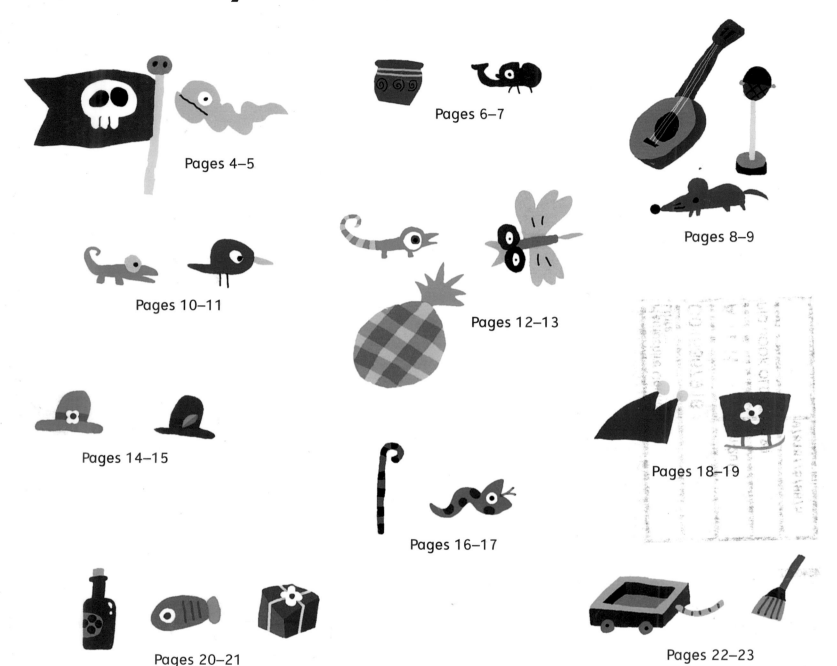

Pages 4–5

Pages 6–7

Pages 8–9

Pages 10–11

Pages 12–13

Pages 14–15

Pages 16–17

Pages 18–19

Pages 20–21

Pages 22–23

Distributed in the UK by Bounce Sales & Marketing
Distributed in Australia by Scholastic Australia
Distributed in New Zealand by Random House NZ

This edition first published in 2013 by Gecko Press
PO Box 9335, Marion Square, Wellington 6141, New Zealand
info@geckopress.com

Original title: *100-nin Kakurembo*
© 2009 Masayuki Sebe

First published in Japan in 2009 by Kaisei-Sha Publishing Co., Ltd, Tokyo
English translation rights arranged with Kaisei-Sha Publishing Co., Ltd.
through the Japan Foreign-Rights Centre

A catalogue record for this book is available from the
National Library of New Zealand

Typesetting by Vida & Luke Kelly, New Zealand
Printed by Everbest, China

ISBN hardback: 978-1-877579-86-8
ISBN paperback: 978-1-877579-87-5

For more curiously good books, visit www.geckopress.com